Dressing Up

Before each ball, the fairies spend a long time preparing their outfits. They carefully sew together layers of pretty petals, and sprinkle them with a little fairy dust.

When you have pressed-out the outfits, carefully fold them over the heads of the fairies. The brighter side of the costume should be on the outside. Then fold over the paper tab to secure the two sides of the outfit together.

Flower Fairies

Paper Dolls

Inspired by Cicely Mary Barker

Dress your paper dolls for the ball!

Inside you'll find four press-out fairies, eight press-out fairy outfits, and some beautiful accessories! There are also two press-out flower lanterns and some beautiful decorations for your ballroom.

Press out the fairies and their outfits, then decide who is going to wear what. When you've finished playing, put all of the pieces into the pocket on the inside (back) cover, until it's time for the next ball.

FREDERICK WARNE

We're going to the Ball!

These four little fairies
have never been to a ball
before, so they're
very excited!

You'll find press-out versions of
these Flower Fairies in the middle
section of the book. There are
lots of outfits for them to wear,
so you can mix and match as
often as you like.

Christmas Tree
Fairy

Ragged
Robin
Fairy

Pear
Blossom
Fairy

Columbine
Fairy

Original Outfits

It's not just little girl fairies who
dress their best for the ball, the boy
fairies have stunning outfits too!

Every fairy costume is unique,
and is made from leaves, flowers,
petals, grasses, and even seeds.
Which of the fairy outfits
do you like the best?

Press out the Flower Fairies, the flower lanterns, and their
stands. Stand each of the Flower Fairies up by inserting the
cuts by their feet into the small cuts in the stand.
Repeat this for the lanterns.

Dress up and Dance!

You're sure to have a wonderful time at the Flower Fairy Ball! All Flower Fairies love to dance.

Dress the four fairies in the outfits you like the most. Then put on some music and let the fairies dance! What music do you think they'll like best? How long will the fairies dance for?

Setting the Scene

The Fairy Ball is one of the highlights of the year, so the fairies like to make the ballroom look especially beautiful!

In the middle pages of this book you'll find two flower lanterns, and on the last page there are some pretty flowers. Press these out and arrange them so that the fairies have a stunning area to dance in.

Fairy Accessories

Accessories are very important to
Flower Fairies, especially when
they're dressing up for a ball! It's the little
details that make an outfit really special.

Press-out the accessories below and place
them on the fairies. There are flower crowns
and hats to wear, and stunning bags to hang
over delicate fairy arms!

Fold the two 'ears' of this
hat towards you, using
the dotted lines as
a guide.

Goodbye for now fairy
friends! Don't forget that
we love balls and parties, so
please come and play with
us again soon!

Lots of love,

The Flower Fairies xxx

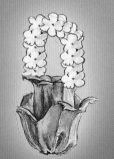